GW00482276

7p

# Emma

## BABY TALKING

SPICE GIRLS
OFFICIAL PUBLICATION

**Research**
Noam Friedlander

**Design**
JMP Ltd

**Photography**
The Spice Girls' families
Ray Burmiston
Brian Rasic
Rankin Waddell
Alex Bailey
Michael Ginsberg

**Spice Girls Management**
Simon Fuller @ 19 Management

**Thanks to**
Catri Drummond
James Freedman
Sally Hudson
Gerrard Tyrrell

First published in 1997 by
**Zone/Chameleon Books**
an imprint of Andre Deutsch Ltd.
a member of the VCI plc Group
106 Great Russell Street
London WCIB 3LJ
in association with19 Management Ltd
Printed in Italy by G. Canale & C. Turin

CIP Data for this title is available from the British Library

**ISBN  0223 99322 3**

**A Zone production**

"Hiya, Spice fans. This is Emma, also known as Baby Spice, welcoming you to my own little book. Thanks for buying my book ~ I bet we have a lot in common so I'm sure you'll enjoy sharing a few of my secrets..."

Emma
xxx

"The first time I appeared on stage was when I was about 3 or 4, and I did a ballet show. I was the swan and wore a big tutu. All the other girls had to dance around me."

"I wouldn't be without my white baby-doll dress. It goes with everything, it's comfortable and it's cool."

"I went abroad quite a lot when I was younger because I used to do catalogue modelling on location – Corsica, Lanzarote, Portugal. From the age of six until I was twelve, I went away every year for two weeks for shoots. It was brilliant, because there used to be about ten kids and we only worked every other day. I was lucky."

"I used to be quite worried about having a real womanly body, but now I think, that's me and I like the way I am."

"I suppose I'm fairly used to the entertainment business. I've been modelling since I was a child and always really loved it. My Mum put the money away for me, and I ended up using it to pay for drama school."

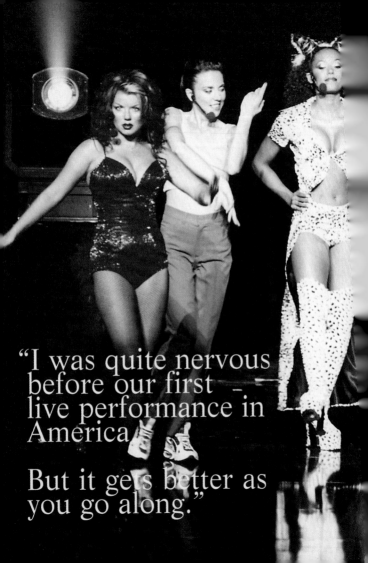

"I was quite nervous before our first live performance in America.

But it gets better as you go along."

"We feel really comfortable on stage – it's a real buzz."

**"I watched** *Grease* **and** *Dirty Dancing* **over and over again. Also, I'm a big fan of** *Pollyanna* **with Hayley Mills, and** *Annie.***"**

"I've got a big double bed with a massive duvet and about six pillows, because I love being really squashy. Sometimes I sleep with my teddies, but sometimes they get on my nerves and I throw them out. I've got lots of teddies, but I only ever have two on my bed."

"When I wear lipstick I often don't wear eye make-up, or I wear eye make-up and no lipstick. You don't have to go mad – just little bits here and there. Natural is best."

"My ambition is for us five to stay happy in the Spice Girls and for me to buy my Mum a house."

"When I first met her, I thought Geri was a **nutter**.

She was wearing short red dungarees with stripey socks and massive shoes."

"When I first met Mel B, I thought she was *incredibly cool*."

"I've got quite a young face, like a lot of girls have, and **too much** make-up can make me look a bit like a dolly."

"I never wore any make-up until I was about fifteen."

"We're doing it girls, so can you. Even if you have to shout a bit louder and go for it."

"I still get goose-pimples whenever I hear one of our songs."

"You learn from everything that's happened to you, especially the bad stuff. Well, you hope you learn from it."

"You can be a strong female and still wear make-up and a WonderBra."

"I always say to friends that they shouldn't take any nonsense from their boyfriends and a lot of them don't. If they feel they're not doing something right, then they'll tell them. You've got to say how you feel because otherwise they'll just carry on doing whatever it is. If you think about it, men prefer that anyway. They don't like a girl who's just a wimp."

"The worst advice
I've ever been
given is,

"Don't do it."

My Mum told me
once that people have
got to learn by their
own mistakes and
she was right."

"I fulfilled a fantasy at the Brits. I've always wanted to wear a very beautiful, long, fitted dress - and I did that night.

I loved it - it was so sexy.

"We were brought up to be strong females and to go whichever way we wanted, with lots of support behind us.

That's Girl Power

– and it's been around a long time."

"I don't know if eating sweet things makes you sweeter - it might do. I think it worked with me!"

"I like
cuddles
and
candy
floss!"

"I'm quite a smile-sweetly-and-flutter-my-eyelashes kind of girl. I'll give him a grin and walk away, then come back a bit later."

" **Girl Power** is about taking control of your life and having respect for other people and yourself. When I first met the Girls I'd been going out with a boy for a long time, but I quickly realised that he wasn't right for me and got rid of him.

That was **Girl Power** in action, right there."

"I never really thought I was any good, so I've always worked really hard at it. I have to keep working for everything I get and I take it all one day at a time."

"When I first met her, I thought Victoria was a bit too posh, but a good friend. The woman I admire most is my Mum because she's a strong female who did her own thing when she and my Dad split. She learnt Karate and now she's a black belt and a Karate teacher. To me she's perfect - a really cool chick. She's always moving forward."

"I didn't start eating donuts until I was 10 or 11."

We used to have donut eating competitions at school - you weren't allowed to lick your lips until you'd finished. I always won! All you had to think was, first eat the donut and then, at the end ...

you've still got all that sugar
around your mouth to lick off!"

"My dreamy donut moment -
sitting in a big pile of them."

"If I was going to pig out on one food it would be Creme Brulée, because I've got a very sweet tooth."

# Thanks for reading my book!

Big
Kisses

Emma
xxx